SECEDER CEMETERY

A Transcription with Photographs

BETTY ELZA

Author's Tranquility Press
ATLANTA, GEORGIA

Copyright © 2023 by BETTY ELZA

All rights reserved. No part of this publication may be reproduced, distributed or transmitted in any form or by any means, including photocopying, recording, or other electronic or mechanical methods, without the prior written permission of the publisher, except in the case of brief quotations embodied in critical reviews and certain other noncommercial uses permitted by copyright law. For permission requests, write to the publisher, addressed "Attention: Permissions Coordinator," at the address below.

BETTY ELZA/Author's Tranquility Press
3800 Camp Creek Pkwy SW Bldg. 1400-116 #1255
Atlanta, GA 30331, USA
www.authorstranquilitypress.com

Ordering Information:
Quantity sales. Special discounts are available on quantity purchases by corporations, associations, and others. For details, contact the "Special Sales Department" at the address above.

SECEDER CEMETERY: A TRANSCRIPTION WITH PHOTOGRAPHS/BETTY ELZA
Hardcover: 978-1-961123-54-0
Paperback: 978-1-961123-55-7
eBook: 978-1-961123-56-4

INTRODUCTION

This transcription is arranged by row and by named lot starting from the circular road entrance at the top of the hill. The reading was done from the bottom of the hill up across the cemetery toward the wooded area, left to right as you would read a book.

Row one and the Cochrane Lot and the Speer Lot are the first listings. Photographs of stones are included for each lot. This arrangement was used to help facilitate research on these families.

Some people refer to old transcriptions of this cemetery as being the most accurate. But two of the old transcriptions of this cemetery, one from 1948 and one from 1963, are incomplete. There are markers in the cemetery with names that are not on these lists. However, they, and others were used for reference in compiling the record presented in this book.

Some researchers have claimed that this cemetery has been vandalized and stones broken. That may or may not be true, but stones here have been damaged. It has suffered because of its age. This two-acre cemetery dates back to 1802. It has been damaged by weather. At least two severe storms caused trees to fall into the cemetery and resulted in broken markers. Another thing that has taken its toll on the cemetery is neglect. But it is very possible that there are no longer family members in the area to maintain some of these lots. Many markers are in disrepair. Undoubtedly, there are burials here for which there are no longer records.

The burial markers are very difficult to read. Every effort was made to get photographs that can be read easily enough to distinguish names, dates, and other markings.

ACKNOWLEDGMENT

Many thanks to Floyd Elza and Lucille Procious for their help with this project.

Seceder Cemetery

Contents

Transcription for Seceder Cemetery

Alternate names for this Cemetery include Union Cemetery, Old Rehobeth Cemetery, and Seceder Cemetery. The cemetery is located at Dillinger's Corners (near Mechanicsville) Clarion Township, Clarion County, Pennsylvania.

GROUP ONE Cochrane / Cochran Lot

COCHRANE, Mary Elvira   b. 21 Aug 1830   d. 17 Nov 1847   17y 2m 27d
    Daughter of John and Catherine Cochrane

COCHRANE, Anna Catherine   b. 21 Sep 1858   d. 2 Sep 1863   4yr 11m 12d
    Daughter of W. F. & S. M. Cochrane

COCHRANE, John   b. 7 Dec 1798   d. 19 Sep 1861   62y 9m 12d

COCHRANE, Joseph   b. 18 Feb 1807   d. 19 Nov 1871   64y 9m 1d

COCHRANE, Mary Catherine   b.   d. 2 Sep 1863   *No Marker*

COCHRANE, Catharine   b. 8 Apr 1800   d. 26 Sep 1885   85y 4m 28d
    Wife of Joseph

COCHRANE, J. M.   b.   d. 1865 188th PA Inf Co 1861-65
    Two other graves in this lot

Mary Elvira Cochrane

Anna Catherine Cochrane
"Suffer little children and forbid them not to come unto me for of such is the kingdom of heaven."

John Cochrane

Joseph Cochrane

Catherine Cochrane

J. M. Cochrane

GROUP TWO Speer Lot

Illegible Stone
SPEER, James	b. 1801	d. 22 Jan 1873	72 y
Sarah (his wife)	b. 1811	d. 2 Feb 1892	81y
SPEER, James, Sr.	b. 18 Dec 1749	d. 18 Jun 1851	101y 6m

Rev War Soldier, Clarion County Chapter, NSDAR, Memorial Marker, 2007

SPEER, George H.	b.	d. No Dates Modern Stone
Samuel	b.	d. No Dates Modern Stone

Illegible Stone

James Speer & Sarah, his wife

James Speer, Sr.

George H. Speer
Samuel Speer

GROUP THREE _____abough Lot

_______abough, Samuel W.   b. 1800   d. 2 Jul 1829   29y

Samuel W. _____abough

GROUP FOUR Williams / Meredith Lot

WILLIAMS, Mark   b. 15 Oct 1774   d. 5 Jun 1849   74y 7m 20d
    Gone Home
    Lettice – 1st wife of Mark Williams   b.   d. 1843   *No Marker*
        She was the daughter of Thomas Meredith
    Sarah Allison – 2nd wife of Mark Williams, buried Zion Baptist Cemetery
        She was the daughter of Tate Hamilton Allison
                    b. 11 Jun 1787   d.
MEREDITH, Thomas   b. 1750   d. 10 Aug 1832
    Rev War Soldier, Clarion County Chapter, NSDAR, Memorial Marker, 2007
Eleanor (Ellen)   b. 1755   d. 24 Dec 1824   *No Marker*
    Wife of Thomas Meredith
His original tombstone is no longer there, but the inscription once read: Thomas Meredith, born 1750, died 10 August 1832. Revolutionary War Soldier. Corp. (This date varies from the date on the memorial marker because this date had not been found when the marker was placed.)

Mark Williams

Thomas Meredith

GROUP FIVE Broken Stone – No Markings

Bottom Part of a Stone - No Markings

GROUP SIX Livingston Lot

LIVINGSTON, Wiliam M.	b. 26 Dec 1838	d. 22 Feb 1843	4y 1m 27d
Son of J. & T. Livingston			

William M. Livingston

GROUP SEVEN Mitchell Lot

MITCHELL, Elizabeth	b. 1758	d. 25 Apr 1827	69y
Consort of William Mitchell			
MITCHELL, Amanda J.	b. 3 Jun 1850	d. 6 Oct 1851	1y 4m 3d
Daughter of J. R. & M. A. Mitchell			
MITCHELL, Margaret	b. 1 Jul 1781	d. 11 Oct 1856	75y 3m 10d
Wife of John Mitchell			
MITCHELL, W. C.	b. 22 May 1850	d. 23 Oct 1851	1y 5m 1d
Son of W. & E. Mitchell			

Three small graves in this lot

Elizabeth Mitchell

Amanda J. Mitchell

Margaret Mitchell

W. C. Mitchell

GROUP EIGHT Kady Lot

KADY, Samuel   b. 1784   d. 12 Nov 1854   70y

Samuel Kady

GROUP NINE Clover Lot

CLOVER, Philip, Sr.   b. 12 Jun 1758   d. 19 May 1830   REV WAR
    Rev War Soldier, Clarion County Chapter, NSDAR, Memorial Marker, 2007
    John Peter b. Prussia, father of Philip Clover, Sr.   *No Marker*
    Catherine (Sharpe) Clover   b. Holland, mother of Philip Clover, Sr.   *No Marker*
CLOVER, Mary (Cooper)   b. 1756   d. 1842
CLOVER, Catherine   b. 22 Mar 1827   d. 22 Apr 1827   1m
CLOVER, Margaret   b. 6 Aug 1844   d. 1 Feb 1846   1y 5m 26d
CLOVER, Frances   b. 27 Jul 1840   d. 8 Aug 1842   2y 12d
CLOVER, Martha   b.   d. 4 Aug 1843   *No Marker*
CLOVER, Isabella (Cathcart)   b. 1818   d. 18 Sep 1886   68y
    2nd Wife of Rev. Philip Clover
CLOVER, Hiram H.   b. 26 Jun 1853   d. 21 Mar 1878   24y 8m 25d
    Son of Isabella and Philip Clover *Gone Home*
CLOVER, Frances   b. 22 Jan 1795   d. 28 Dec 1837   42y 11m 6d
    1st Wife of Rev. Philip Clover
CLOVER, Rev. Philip, Jr.   b. 6 Jun 1795   d. 12 Apr 1888   92y 10m 6d
CLOVER, John   b. 1853   d. 1878
    Son of Isabella and Philip Clover

Philip Clover

Mary (Cooper) Clover

Catherine Clover

Margaret Clover

Frances Clover

Isabella (Cathcart) Clover

Hiram H. Clover
This stone was refurbished in recent years.

Frances Clover

Rev. Philip Clover

John Clover

GROUP TEN Jones Lot

JONES, Peter   b. 17 Apr 1752   d. 27 May 1829   77y
   Rev War Soldier, Clarion County Chapter, NSDAR, Memorial Marker, 2007
JONES, Rebecca (Scott)   b. 1759   d. 27 Jun 1832 Mother   73y
JONES, Rebecca – 1st wife of John Jones   b.   d. 20 Mar 1831
JONES, John   b. 10 Feb 1781   d. 24 Dec 1858   77y 10m 14d
JONES, Catharine (Clover)   b. 2 Sep 1783   d. 14 Sep 1851   68y 12d
   Consort of John Jones – 2nd wife of John Jones

Peter Jones

Rebecca (Scott) Jones

Rebecca Jones, First Wife of John

John Jones

Catherine (Clover) Jones

GROUP ELEVEN Port Lot

PORT, Ann   b. 8 Jan 1837   d. 29 Mar 1842   5y 2m 21d
    Daughter of Henry & Rebecca (Clover) Port
PORT, Margaret Ann   b. 31 Oct 1843   d. 16 Jan 1846   2y 2m 16d
PORT, John Q.   b. 10 Jun 1849   d. 6 Jul 1851   2y 26d
    Son of Henry & Rebecca (Clover) Port
PORT, Lawellen   b. 22 May 1851   d. 1 Dec 1851   6m 9d
    Son of Henry & Rebecca (Clover) Port

Ann Port

Margaret Ann Port

John Q. Port

Lawellen Port

Illegible Stone Propped Against a Tree

GROUP TWELVE Mc Garrah / Mc Garra Lot

MC GARRAH Robert Alaxander b. 26 Mar 1825   d. 26 Jun 1825   3m

MC GARRAH, Eleanor (McCain) b. 1793   d. 6 Jan 1827   34y
    Consort of Joseph McGarrah

MC GARRAH, Huldah*   b. 1820-1822   d. Nov 1826   4-6y

MC GARRAH, Son of Joseph and Eleanor   b. 7 Feb 1823 d. 9 Feb 1823   2d

MC GARRAH, Joseph   b. 26 Mar 1825   d. 26 Jun 1825   3m *No Marker*
    Supposedly, there was a marker here at one time for Eleanor, twin of Joseph

MC GARRAH, Rev. Alexander   b.   d. 26 Jun 1825   *No Marker*

Robert Alaxander Mc Garrah

Eleanor Mc Garrah

Huldah Mc Garrah

Son of Joseph & Eleanor

Huldah's epitaph
*Remember friends as you pass by, As you are now, such was I.
As I am now so you must be. Prepare for death and follow me.*

GROUP THIRTEEN Corbett Lot

CORBETT, Theodore	b. 4 Apr 1835	d. 4 Feb 1837	1y 10m
Son of S. T. & P. Corbett			
CORBETT, William	b. 16 Jun 1751	d. 16 May 1831	80y
Rev War Soldier, Clarion County Chapter, NSDAR, Memorial Marker, 2007			
CORBETT, Sarah Bloom (Clover)	b. 1756	d. 25 Nov 1828	72y
Wife of William Corbett, daughter of John Peter Clover			
CORBETT, John Clover	b. 30 May 1781	d. 30 Mar 1853	74y 5m 1d
DUNLAP, Margaret	b. 20 Sep 1788	d. 20 Apr 1817	28y 7m
Wife of William Dunlap			
MAXWELL, Robert	b. 1768	d. 17 Mar 1847	79y
Ann (His wife)	b. 1786	d. 15 Jul 1822	36y

Theodore Corbett

The following stones for William Corbett and Sarah Corbett were lying on the ground against a tree in 2007, but they have been righted.

William Corbett

Sarah Bloom (Clover) Corbett

John C. Corbett

Margaret Dunlap

Robert Maxwell & Wife Ann

GROUP FOURTEEN Allison Lot

ALLISON, Tate Hamilton   b. 1759   d. 1850   *No Marker*
   Rev War Soldier, Clarion County Chapter, NSDAR, Memorial Marker, 2007
   He was born in Cumberland County, PA and died after the 1850 Census.
   Mary "Polly" (Henry) Wife of Tate Hamilton Allison   *No Marker*

Tate Hamilton Allison

GROUP FIFTEEN Galbraith Lot

GALBRAITH, Caroline (Clover)   b. 3 Nov 1796   d. 3 Jun 1818   21y 7m
Wife of William Galbraith

Caroline (Clover) Galbraith

GROUP SIXTEEN Mc Camant / Mc Cammant / Mc Cormick Lot

MC CAMMANT, Walker   b. 21 Apr 1841   d. 25 Oct 1845   4y 6m 4d
   Son of J. G. & M. Mc Cammant
MC CAMMANT, John M.   b. 4 Jan 1836   d. 4 Jul 1840   4y 6m
   Son of J. G. & M. Mc Cammant
MC CAMMANT, Amantha J.   b. 3 Sep 1831   d. 3 Jul 1840   8y 10m
   Daughter of J. G. & M. Mc Cammant
MC CORMICK, Jasper N.   b. 30 Apr 1838   d. 7 Dec 1840   2y 7m 7d
   Son of H. & S.
A. M.   b. 1743   d. 15 Jul 1829   86y

Walker McCammant

John M. McCammant

Amantha J. McCammant

Jasper N. McCormick

A. M.

This fieldstone for A. M.
is next to the Corbett Lot.

GROUP SEVENTEEN Guthrie Lot

GUTHRIE, John   b. 23 Dec 1774   d. 23 Sep 1839   64y 9m
GUTHRIE, Jane (Maffett)   b. 1769   d. 18 Jul 1833   64y
She was exemplary in her life, and died in full hope of a happy immortality. "What thou art reading on my stone, I oft have read on other stones. And others soon will read of thee what they are reading now of me." (L. Hull-Blairsville)
GUTHRIE, John M   b. 22 May 1798   d.
GUTHRIE, Joseph   b. 11 Jun 1808   d. 16 Jul 1808

John Guthrie

Jane Guthrie

John M. Guthrie

Joseph Guthrie

Note: There is a Spanish American War marker on the grave of John Guthrie, but he could not have served. He died in 1839 before the war.

These stones for John M. and Joseph Guthrie are lying against a tree in the Potter Lot.

GROUP EIGHTEEN Wilson Lot

MAFFETT, Nancy E.	b. d. 3 May 183 – Wife of John Maffett		26y 5m 9d
WILSON, Sarah (McConnell)	b. 1782	d. 25 Mar 1823	41y

Wife of Robert Wilson Grandparents of Judge Theo Wilson

WILSON, Robert	b. 1774	d. 21 May 1832	58y
WILSON, Nancy	b. 1794	d. 1798	4y

In memory of Nancy Wilson, infant daughter of Samuel and Jean Love Wilson, who died and was buried at sea in 1798. She left Ardstraw, County Tyrone, Ireland in the year 1798 to accompany her parents to the U.S.A. She died and was buried at sea.

WILSON, John	b. 1791	d. 1841	Veteran, War of 1812

He served his country in the War of 1812

Uncle of Judge Theo Wilson

Nancy E. Maffett

Sarah Wilson

Robert Wilson

John Wilson

Nancy Wilson

GROUP NINETEEN Roll Lot

ROLL, John, Jr.   b. 12 Jan 1755   d. 15 Jan 1816
    Pvt. 7th Company, 8th Battalion, Cumberland Co, PA under Captain Robert Means, REV WAR DAR marker on stone
Mary (Frampton)   b. 1757   d. 1822   *No Marker*
ROLL, John, Sr.   b. 7 Apr 1734   d. 17 Jan 1815
    He may be buried in Anderson Cemetery in Jefferson County, PA where he lived before coming to Clarion County, PA
Mary (Wife of John Roll, Sr.)   *No Marker*
ROLL – FULTON Memorial Stone

Fulton, Agnes 1750-1826	John Roll, Sr. 1743*-1814
Fulton, Henry	Roll, Mary
Fulton, Cochran 1782-1853	Roll, John, Jr. 1755-1816
Fulton, Nancy (Roll) 1792-1865	Roll, Mary (Frampton) 1757-1822

*This date is transposed 1743 instead of 1734. If John Roll, Sr. had been born in 1743, he would have been twelve when his son John was born in 1755.

John Roll

Roll - Fulton Memorial Stone

GROUP TWENTY Whitman Lot

WHITMAN, Smith   b. 30 Sep 1846   d. 17 Dec 1923
  He was once the caretaker of the cemetery and asked to be buried here.
  His was the last interment in this cemetery.

Modern stone

Smith Whitman

GROUP TWENTY-ONE Williams Lot

Broken Stone - Illegible

WILLIAMS, Joseph   b. 1805   d. 2 Feb 1850   45y
  Father of John Williams, grandfather of the Smathers brothers in Limestone and Mrs.
  Margaret Port

Joseph Williams

GROUP TWENTY-TWO Gibson Lot

GIBSON, Jane   b. 3 Dec 1806   d. 16 Aug 1880   74y 8m 13d
GIBSON, William   b. 1756   d. 12 Jan 1816   60y
GIBSON, Margaret   b. 21 Oct 1784   d. 11 Dec 1868   84y 7m 21d

Jane Gibson

William Gibson

Margaret Gibson

GROUP TWENTY-THREE Potter Lot

POTTER, Eli	b. 1809	d. 20 Jun 1832	23y
Illegible Stone			
Fieldstone No Markings			
POTTER, Adam	b. 1814	d. 20 Jan 1834	20y
POTTER, Robert E.	b. 18 Jun 1833	d. 14 May 1834	10m 26d
Son of John and Nancy (Thompson) Potter			
POTTER, Leburn H.	b.	d. 12 Aug 1843	
Son of James and Rhoda (Williams) Potter			
POTTER, James	b. 1766	d. 14 Feb 1855	89y
U. S. Service			
POTTER, Mary (McFadden)	b. 1767	d. 4 Oct 1819	45y
Wife of James Potter			
POTTER, James	b. 1800	d. 15 Nov 1809	9y
Son of James and Mary Potter			
POTTER, James M.	b. 1826	d. 20 Feb 1836	10y
Son of John and H. Potter			
MC CORNELL, John	b.	d. Jun 1842	*No Marker* 43y
Adam	b.	d. 21 Jun 1842	43y 4m 15d

One other grave here, part of a broken marker

Eli Potter

Illegible Stone

Fieldstone – No Markings

Adam Potter

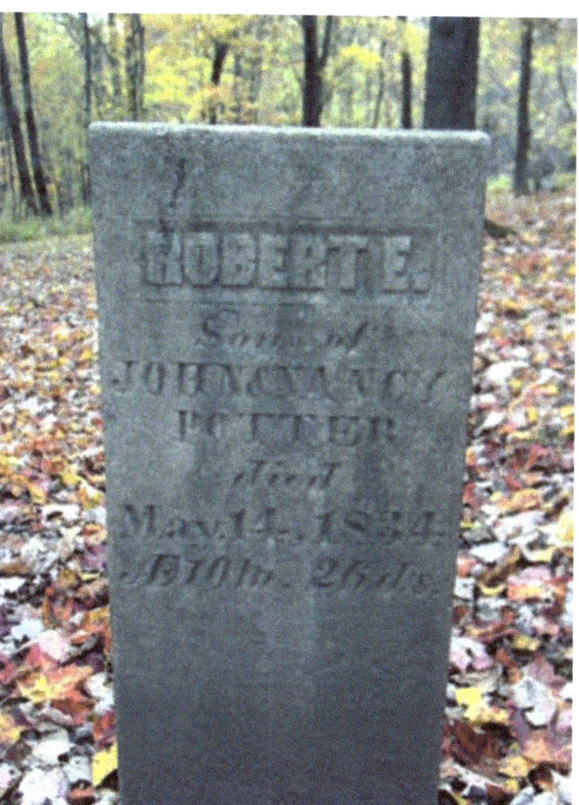

Robert E. Potter

Leburn H. Potter

James Potter

Mary (McFadden) Potter

James Potter

GROUP TWENTY-FOUR Broken Illegible Stones

GROUP TWENTY-FIVE George Lot

GEORGE, Samuel   b. 13 Mar 1810   d. 10 Aug 1884   74y 4m 28d
Sarah (His Wife)   b.   d.

The small modern marker was placed between 2007-2010. Usually, flowers, such as the ones here, adorn this grave by early summer each year.

Samuel George

Markers Not Located

There are two names on a transcription list for 1999 at the Clarion County Historical Society for which no markers could be located. They are George Flack who died 17 October 1857 and Margaret Ross who died 26 August 1846. She was the wife of Robert and was 56 years old.

Oldest Legible Markers

The oldest marker that is legible today is that of Joseph Guthrie, who was born and died in 1808. The next ones are the Potters. James Potter died in 1809 and Mary in 1812. Although, Judge Peter Clover said the earliest burial was James McFadin (christened Paul) Clover, who was the son of Philip and Sarah Roll Clover. He said they were buried here, too.

GROUP TWENTY-SIX Unidentified Lot

Broken Stone – No Markings

Revolutionary War Patriots

There are several Revolutionary War soldiers and patriots buried in this cemetery. Clarion County Chapter, National Society Daughters of the American Revolution put memorial markers on their graves in 2007, as they did the other known graves of Revolutionary War patriots in the county. The following are the soldiers whose graves were marked in this cemetery: Tate Hamilton Allison, William Corbett, Peter Jones, Thomas Meredith, and James Speer. The graves of Philip Clover and John Roll had been marked previously by family members. A history of the patriots buried in Clarion County and three surrounding counties is documented in the book, Revolutionary War Patriots of Clarion, Jefferson, Armstong, and Venango Counties, PA. Copies are available from the author by calling 814-764-3423.

Directions to the Cemetery

From Exit 64 (old Exit 10 – Clarion / New Bethlehem) off Interstate 80, go south on State Route 66 one-fourth of a mile. A stone with the name of the cemetery inscribed is on the left side of the highway. Turn left and take the unpaved lane up the hill to the cemetery.

Seceder Cemetery

Bequest for Cemetery Maintenance

A bequest of Judge T. L. Wilson, great, great grandson of Jean Wilson, provides for basic maintenance, such as mowing and basic clean-up of tree debris. People are welcome to visit the cemetery to pay their respects to those buried there.

Recorders

This cemetery was walked by Lucille Procious and Betty Elza on 17 August 2007 and this record made. It has been updated with recent photographs through October 2010.

INDEX

www.ingramcontent.com/pod-product-compliance
Lightning Source LLC
Chambersburg PA
CBHW041051050726
47599CB00018B/2110